Also by Giles A. Lutz:

THE BLEEDING LAND
THE GOLDEN LAND
WILD RUNS THE RIVER
THE MAGNIFICENT FAILURE
THE LONELY RIDE
THE UNBEATEN
THE OFFENDERS
THE GRUDGE
STAGECOACH TO HELL
THE STUBBORN BREED
NIGHT OF THE CATTLEMEN
THE SHOOT OUT
THE TURN AROUND
LURE OF THE OUTLAW TRAIL
THE ECHO
KILLER'S TRAIL
THE GREAT RAILROAD WAR

THIEVES' BRAND